This book belongs to _____

Also Available in the Rosenburg Riding Stables Series:
Antonia, the Horse Whisperer

Original edition © 2012 Coppenrath Verlag GmbH & Co. KG, Münster, Germany.
Original title: *Reiterhof Rosenburg: Antonia großes Turnier* (ISBN 978-3-8157-5119-0). All rights reserved.
First English-language edition published by Sky Pony Press, 2014.

English Translation Copyright © 2014 by Skyhorse Publishing, Inc.

Sky Pony Press books may be purchased in bulk at special discounts for sales promotion, corporate gifts, fund-raising, or educational purposes. Special editions can also be created to specifications. For details, contact the Special Sales Department, Sky Pony Press, 307 West 36th Street, 11th Floor, New York, NY 10018 or info@skyhorsepublishing.com.

Sky Pony® is a registered trademark of Skyhorse Publishing, Inc.®, a Delaware corporation.

Visit our website at www.skyponypress.com.

10 9 8 7 6 5 4 3 2 1

Manufactured in China, April 2014
This product conforms to CPSIA 2008

Library of Congress Cataloging-in-Publication Data
Zöller, Elisabeth, 1945- author.
 [Antonias grosses Turnier. English]
 Antonia and the big competition / Elisabeth Zöller & Brigitte Kolloch ; illustrated by Betina Gotzen-Beek ; translated from the German by Connie Stradling Morby. -- First English-language edition.
  pages cm. -- (Rosenburg Riding Stables ; volume 2)
 Originally published in German by Coppenrath F in 2012 under title: Antonias grosses Turnier.
 Summary: As the youngest rider in her first show-jumping competition, ten-year-old Antonia struggles to overcome her fear.
 ISBN 978-1-62873-597-0 (hardback)
 [1. Horses--Fiction. 2. Horse shows--Fiction. 3. Fear--Fiction.] I. Kolloch, Brigitte, author. II. Gotzen-Beek, Betina, illustrator.
III. Morby, Connie Stradling, translator. IV. Title.
 PZ7.Z74Ak 2014
 [Fic]--dc23
       2014002135
ISBN: 978-1-62873-597-0

Cover art by Betina Gotzen-Beek

Ebook ISBN: 978-1-62873-946-6

Elisabeth Zöller & Brigitte Kolloch

Antonia
and the Big Competition

Illustrations by
Betina Gotzen-Beek

Translated from the German by
Connie Stradling Morby

Sky Pony Press
New York

Horse Currying

Antonia was looking into her school bag again to see if she had packed everything she needed for the day when Karen, the kind-hearted soul of the Rosenburg household, called from the kitchen: "Breakfast! Caroline, Antonia, hurry up, please! It's getting late!"

Antonia jumped down the stairs. Her two favorite horses, Elfin Dance and Snow White, were waiting, after all.

Twenty minutes later, when she bounded into the row of stalls, her father had already finished giving out the feed.

"Good morning, Papa," said Antonia, giving her father a big kiss.

"Hello, Antonia. Did you sleep well?"

Antonia nodded and took the grooming kit from the ground.

"Elfin Dance! Snow White!"

The two horses were standing next to each other in

their stalls; Elfin Dance, her long-legged chestnut gelding with the stripe, and Snow White, her gray horse.

The two horses really couldn't have been any more different, she thought. Just like every morning during the last six weeks since Elfin Dance had come to their stables, a broad smile crept across Antonia's face. She stroked their necks and backs and ran her hand tenderly through their manes; first Snow White's and then Elfin Dance's. Snow White snorted softly, as if she were trying to call Antonia's name. Her nostrils snuggled into Antonia's hand.

Elfin Dance, on the other hand, whinnied energetically and pranced impatiently in place. "Let's go. When are you going to get here?" he seemed to be saying.

Antonia put halters on both of them and led them out.

"Come, Snow White. Elfin Dance, don't push like that. We're going right to the grooming area."

The morning sun was already sending down its luminous rays, bathing the farm in bright light. Antonia tied Elfin Dance and Snow White next to each other on the hooks on the barn wall. Elfin Dance's coat glistened like polished wood in the sun. Even though Snow White's coat stood up shaggily in a few places, she was the more good-natured of the two. Antonia began the grooming with her. She brushed the horse's head and neck and then went over her back. Snow White enjoyed it so much that she snorted softly.

"This evening, my love, we'll go for a ride again with Leona and Caroline. I'm so glad that your leg is better after the accident."

Then Elfin Dance piped up, requesting Antonia's attention. "And you, you wild thing, weren't we lucky that Mr. Bonhumeur left you and Asseem with us here at the farm. When I think about that thunderstorm that almost ruined everything, I still get butterflies in my stomach! Mr. Bonhumeur wanted to take you right back to France."

Mr. Bonhumeur was a horse enthusiast from France. Maria, Antonia's aunt—who had a feeling for outstanding horses and a practiced eye—had bought several horses for him at auction. For a few weeks he had been having two of them train at the Rosenburg farm. One of them was Asseem. He was to be trained by Antonia's older sister, Caroline, with the help of Mr. Sonnenfeld, the riding instructor at the farm. The other horse was Elfin Dance. Mr. Bonhumeur had been so impressed with Antonia's calm and loving way with Elfin Dance that he had insisted that she train him with the best riding instructor in the area, Mr. Hegemann.

"For my little girl and my prized horse, only the best training," he had specified in a thick French accent. "Then my Elfin Dance stays here on Rosenburg Farm."

Antonia got a finishing brush for cleaning and smoothing the horses' coats and gave Elfin Dance's back an encouraging pat with the flat of her hand.

"Our lessons with Mr. Hegemann are really fun for me." She looked into Elfin Dance's eyes. "Sometimes I think we'll do it all. I can hardly wait for this afternoon's lesson."

Just then Mr. Sonnenfeld passed by. "Hi, Antonia. Wow, you're here with your horses so early every morning."

"Good morning, Mr. Sonnenfeld. That goes without saying." She gave Snow White and Elfin Dance a nudge.

"Yes, but you do it all before school," he said appreciatively.

"School! Oh crud! I completely forgot! We're having a vocabulary test today!" Why was that just crossing her mind now? "I'd better get a move on."

"If you'd said that yesterday afternoon, I could have quizzed you on your vocabulary," said Mr. Sonnenfeld.

"At least I know what 'horse' means! And that's the most important vocabulary word of all!" Antonia smiled. "It's really exciting: fifth grade, new school, and new teachers. I'm glad that Leona sits next to me, because I don't know any of the other kids in the class very well. Leona is really the best friend ever."

And even though she still did want to study her vocabulary, she kept chatting, and Mr. Sonnenfeld listened. "English with Mrs. Warner is great, but math with the math codfish is even more fun." Then Antonia took carrots out of her pocket and gave them to both horses. "That's what we call Mr. Fischbach because he has such a wide mouth—like a cod." She giggled.

"That's not nice," said Mr. Sonnenfeld.

"He doesn't know," answered Antonia. "But do you know what Leona and I really have trouble with? The huge building! You can't imagine it; our indoor riding arena could get swallowed up inside it. We're always getting lost. So, I really need to get going now. Bye, Mr. Sonnenfeld."

"Bye, Antonia. I'll keep my fingers crossed for your vocabulary test."

Antonia took Snow White and Elfin Dance back to their stalls and said good-bye to both of them. She was just about to run into the kitchen when Mr. Sonnenfeld stopped her again. "Can you help this afternoon with currying and storing the hay? Felix is still sick. Caroline and John are helping out, too."

"Sure," called Antonia. She ran to the breakfast table and gulped her bread and jam under Karen's disapproving eye.

"Child, you have to eat a sensible breakfast, not always so rushed and on the way to the bus."

But Antonia didn't hear her because she was already hurrying along the road to the bus stop.

The bus was approaching her stop.

"Hello, Leona!" she called and flopped into the empty seat next to her friend. "Can you quiz me on the vocabulary words? And then I'll quiz you . . ."

"Hey, little girl! Are you still trying not to fall off your horse?" rang out a voice from the back of the bus. Alina! Alina Senger! What was she doing on the bus?

"I haven't seen you at a competition in a long time. Have you given up competing?" Alina sneered.

But Antonia had won the last summer competition ahead of Alina. She probably couldn't stand it. Antonia turned around slowly; Alina was sitting there with her friends, grinning nastily right in Antonia's face.

"What's with that?" asked Leona.

Antonia just rolled her eyes. "You know Alina Senger! She's such a pain. Just because she's twelve, she thinks she can do everything better—ride faster and jump farther and higher. But I won last time. Nah, she always has an excuse in store. Either her horse had a bad day or she was blinded by the sun."

But Antonia suspected that now Alina would be making her life at school difficult, too.

Hard Training

After eating lunch in the kitchen, Antonia and Caroline helped Mr. Sonnenfeld; then Antonia got Elfin Dance out of the stall and saddled him.

"Hello, my beauty. Do you think we'll make it through the hurdles again today?" she asked.

Yesterday they hadn't been bad; it was only on the last hurdle that they had needed three approaches. The closer the riding lesson got, the more excited Antonia became.

At exactly three o'clock, she was standing in the indoor riding arena with Elfin Dance, greeting Mr. Hegemann warmly. It was still something special to get lessons from such a well-known riding instructor. When Antonia thought back to their first riding lesson, she had to smile. After all, not only did Mr. Hegemann have a reputation for being an outstanding riding instructor, but he was also known for his strictness and discipline. At the same time, he gave all riders and horses their freedom. For him, a great intimacy between the two was the basis for every riding success. He usually trained the best-known dressage and jumper riders!

"Be honest! Trust yourself! You'll accomplish what you want." That's what Mr. Hegemann's lessons were based on. Under his guidance, Antonia was proud to sit up straight in the saddle, to stride out the show jumping course carefully, or to do a good jump.

By now Antonia liked Mr. Hegemann so much that Caroline and Leona often teased her by saying, "You're in love with him!"

Antonia would blush and just yell, "Nonsense! You two are crazy! He's just a great teacher . . ."

Mr. Hegemann's voice made her snap out of her daydream. "Let him walk on a long rein," he requested.

Antonia let Elfin Dance warm up.

How easily he ran!

"Trot."

Antonia sat down in the saddle and let Elfin Dance trot. She moved up and down with the motion of the horse to take the strain off his back.

"Great," Mr. Hegemann praised. "Antonia, you stand in the stirrups so lightly. Elfin Dance is loosened up nicely. You have to trust him; you can't be afraid."

"I'm not afraid, Mr. Hegemann," Antonia laughed.

"No, when you ride Elfin Dance, you certainly aren't afraid. But you want to jump. And for that, mutual trust is the most important thing of all," Mr. Hegemann said.

"Now, go backwards, please, even if Elfin Dance doesn't like it. He has to trust you as well and do what you ask him to do," Mr. Hegemann instructed.

Elfin Dance obeyed, even though he didn't really like going backwards.

Finally they fell into a gallop.

"Wonderful!" Antonia praised him.

Mr. Hegemann had set up a show jumping course outside with five hurdles about two feet high. Antonia had to clear each of these now in a curve in three, four, and five strides. Would she get the hang of shifting her weight today?

Antonia started the course. Powerfully and confidently Elfin Dance took each hurdle, and he managed the curves easily.

Now, it was time for the takeoff again! She held her back as straight as possible, letting her hands go forward so that Elfin Dance could stretch out his neck and take off with force.

But this time the upper pole fell down.

"Not so bad, Elfin Dance. At the next hurdle it'll go better. Just keep going," Antonia encouraged him.

They galloped to the next hurdle. Elfin Dance took off, his forehand went up, and at the same time he pushed his nose forward. Antonia extended her arms and stood in the stirrups.

Her sight was directed ahead toward the goal so she could land successfully and then keep moving forward. This time the pole stayed put.

"Excellent job, Antonia and Elfin Dance!" Mr. Hegemann beamed. Antonia hummed, pleased with the praise.

"That's enough for today. I'd like to discuss something else with you, Antonia."

Curious about what Mr. Hegemann wanted from her, Antonia, singing softly, led Elfin Dance to the grooming area. She'd also picked that up from Mr.

Hegemann—singing and humming to the horse. That was good for breathing. But above all, cheerful songs brought pep and a good mood to both her and the horse, so that afterwards Antonia greeted everyone she bounded into with a laugh.

If only her mother could see her now, Antonia thought sometimes, she would be so delighted! But her mother was no longer alive. She had died in an accident when Antonia was three.

Antonia felt impatient waiting for Mr. Hegemann to approach her. With a curious feeling of anticipation in her stomach, Antonia unsaddled Elfin Dance and rubbed him dry.

Finally Mr. Hegemann walked up to her. "Antonia, we've been training now for six weeks, and I think you've made great progress. Certainly you've read that in ten days the Great Riding and Jumping Tournament is being held in Tostedt. Do you feel confident enough to compete riding Elfin Dance? You'll ride in L class."

"I'm in L?" Antonia asked. She had to stop for breath first and then looked wide-eyed at Mr. Hegemann. That meant jumps between three-and-a-half and four feet! She also knew that the competition in Tostedt was one of the most challenging of the season. Suddenly her heart was pounding.

"Do you really think Elfin Dance and I can manage a competition like that? I'm only ten years old after all," she babbled.

"Yes, I think so," Mr. Hegemann answered with an encouraging smile. "Otherwise I wouldn't ask you. Besides, I have a reputation I could lose!" Then he laughed. "You see," he continued, "you're eligible to enter because you already have the class three and four qualification levels. Of course, we don't have much time, but your father agrees that we can put in a few additional hours over the weekend. For Elfin Dance, it'll be the very first competition of his life! But I already have an idea about how we can get him used to the competition atmosphere. What do you think about having various noises coming over the loudspeaker in the indoor riding arena during our next lesson?"

"You mean music and voices talking? People cheering and clapping?" Antonia asked. "I read about that kind of training method once in the horse magazine."

"That's it exactly. I'm sure that's the best way to get him ready. But can you manage all of this along with school, Antonia?"

She didn't give it a second thought. After all, she was getting along fine in her new school.

"That's pretty daring of you," she said, smiling at Mr. Hegemann. "You're taking a big chance on me." Antonia blushed and felt quite proud.

Mr. Hegemann gave her shoulder an encouraging pat. Then he said good-bye and left.

"What do you say?" Antonia asked Elfin Dance. She still had doubts. But if Mr. Hegemann thought she could handle the competition, then she would believe so, too.

Just then, Leona zoomed onto the farm on her bike. As she braked, gravel flew on all sides. Antonia ran up to her and, before Leona could say anything, Antonia burst out, "Get this! Mr. Hegemann just asked me if I'd like to enter the Great Riding and Jumping Tournament."

Leona's eyes widened. "Wow," she shouted, "that's awesome! I've always said, with Elfin Dance, you'll be the best show jumping rider in the world. Cool!" And she grabbed her friend and danced around the farm with her, Leona with her short-cropped blonde hair and freckled snub nose and Antonia with her long, flying hair.

"Now, let's get our homework done quickly so we can go for a ride!" shouted Leona.

It was always fun to do homework with Leona.

"Who can work out the problems the fastest?" Antonia shouted, and they got going for all they were worth. At first, half of their answers were wrong, but they'd had a lot of fun. And after Leona had corrected Antonia's homework and Antonia had corrected Leona's, finally their answers were right. They quizzed each other on vocabulary and read each other their essays.

"Finished! On to the horses!" Leona announced, and the girls dashed to the stable.

They could see through the window that Caroline was coming to the stable also.

Caroline saddled Asseem, Leona got Thunder out of the stall, and Antonia rode her mare Snow White.

Fortunately, the mare's leg was well-healed after a tendon tear; she just would never be able to jump again. But Antonia was happy enough that she could take her out for a ride on a regular basis. After all, Snow White had been her first important horse.

They had just left the farm and had turned off onto the road leading to the woods when Caroline, who had kept turning around, said, "So, nobody can hear us here. We haven't thought at all about Papa's fortieth birthday, which is a week from Sunday."

"Oh my goodness," groaned Antonia. Of course she already had a gift for her father, but with all the excitement of the last few weeks, she had completely forgotten that they should have a special celebration for his fortieth birthday.

"What do you think of a surprise party?" Caroline continued. "Papa should have a good time on his birthday."

"Super idea!" shouted Leona. "I'll ask my mom if she'll make her famous strawberry punch. Nobody can

whip up a delicious strawberry punch like my mother—with alcohol for the grown-ups and without for us." Then she hesitated and looked questioningly at Caroline. "Um, we're invited too, right?"

"Of course," Caroline said. "Grandma will certainly bake a cake, and Grandpa and Mr. Sonnenfeld will handle the grilling. We'll help Karen and Maria with the salad and decorate the farm with candles and strands of lights! Maybe we can even perform a little play or give a speech. What do you think? That would be great!"

"I can't help all that much," Antonia reminded them somewhat sheepishly.

"It doesn't matter that you can't help much. Get ready for your competition! I think a small victory like a sixth or seventh place win would be the most fantastic present for Papa. We'll do the rest," Caroline answered.

"So, whom do you want to invite? If it's supposed to be a surprise party, we have to do it secretly," said Leona.

"Let's think it over—so, your parents and your brother, Jonathan, naturally; John and Felix; Dr. Kemper; Mr. Hegemann . . ." The list grew longer and longer.

And the longer the list got, the more Antonia's stage fright grew. Because when she came home from the competition on Papa's birthday, all eyes would be on her.

Suddenly she said loudly and clearly, the way Mr. Hegemann had taught her, "Never fear! I accept the challenge."

Leona clapped. She knew that Antonia had regained her confidence.

Slowly the three of them rode along the edge of the woods back to the Rosenburg Farm with the manor house, the big longhouse, Grandma and Grandpa's little house, and, behind it, the moat, which used to surround the farm completely back when Rosenburg Farm was still a real castle. But the front part had been drained for a long time.

Dusk was falling. It was late summer, fog was hanging over the harvested fields, and the leaves were slowly changing colors.

Caroline shivered. "It's getting colder," she said.

"And getting dark earlier," Leona said.

"But there are great adventures ahead of us!" shouted Antonia.

An Anxious Week

All week long Antonia trained during every spare minute.

"Will I be able to do it?" Antonia sat in the saddle and let Elfin Dance run in the paddock. One jump still wasn't going right. But she wanted him to succeed. Encouragingly she whispered to Elfin Dance, "Go on. We'll get it."

But she just landed on the ground again, right in front of Caroline's feet. Caroline was sitting on the paddock fence, poring over a notebook.

"Have you thought of anything else for Papa's party?" Caroline asked, lost in thought. She completely ignored Antonia's fall.

"Costume concours d'élégance—riding in costume," Antonia said curtly.

Caroline hugged her. "That's a brilliant idea. I bet we can borrow costumes from the theater; they have old ones. I read that in the newspaper."

Antonia and Caroline whispered for a while longer, planning, giggling, and tittering, until Alexander Rosenburg, who had been watching them from the farm for a while, had had enough.

"Say, what's going on here, anyway?"

"Absolutely secret." Caroline held her finger in front of her mouth.

"Just like a couple of hens." Her father shook his head, laughing.

Antonia climbed into the saddle to repeat the failed jump.

"Antonia." Her father stopped her. "I've wanted to tell you this all along. It's definitely an honor that Mr. Hegemann is sending you to such a competition with Elfin Dance. But don't forget the Olympic Creed: taking part is what counts!" Her father nudged her. "Do you understand that, my girl?"

"Yes, of course, Papa," Antonia laughed.

✳

At the following training session, she practiced the wide view with Mr. Hegemann, the "panorama view," as he called it. "You must always look ahead to the next goal and over the next hurdle. If your eye gets stuck on the ground in front of the bar, then, guaranteed, you'll land there, too."

And—*plop*—Antonia was lying on the ground.

"Crud," she complained, rubbed her behind, gave a quick laugh, and jumped back into the saddle.

"Look farther ahead!" Mr. Hegemann shouted. "Lift your head. Look at the next goal. You'll get it!"

But I still have to look at the rail, thought Antonia. And *splat,* she was down again, but picked herself up quickly, and laughed again. "Pretty hard when you're only allowed to look in the distance."

"Not true at all," Mr. Hegemann said. "You have to keep both in view, what's close and what's in the distance."

Then it got better. Antonia jumped, she walked, and she galloped, always keeping her eye on both the far-off goal and the nearby one.

Although the training was very hard, for Antonia it was also incredibly fun. Was it because of Mr. Hegemann's reassuring words, the courage he instilled in her? Or was it because of Elfin Dance and his for-ward-surging strength?

Elfin Dance was sweating.

"Is he getting a fever?" Antonia asked, concerned.

"No." Mr. Hegemann put his arm around Antonia. "He's just exerted himself a lot, like you. Only Elfin Dance doesn't brood about whether or not he does it.

He's bursting with strength and self-confidence." He added, "Elfin Dance is a brilliant horse, and you are a terrific rider."

"Well . . ." Antonia said.

Elfin Dance nudged her tenderly with his nostrils, and Antonia led him to the stall.

"Wow, Elfin Dance," whispered Antonia. At that moment she noticed great intimacy growing between her and the horse.

Then Caroline arrived with a list of suggested costumes she wanted to get from the theater. "How about a witch costume for Leona?"

"Hey, I'd like a magician's cloak!" shouted Antonia. "Abracadabra, away to the competition," she whispered conspiratorially, waving an imaginary magic wand.

*

On Tuesday before practice Mr. Hegemann said, "After today, we have to go easy on you and Elfin Dance. The two extra lessons on Saturday were very demanding. You both need your strength for the competition and not for the practice jumps. That's why we're only going to do smaller jumps today. Elfin Dance has mastered the big ones. And you even more so."

Antonia nodded in agreement.

Mr. Hegemann smiled. "So, today and tomorrow we'll concentrate on strategy. Let an old hand like me explain something important to you: you ride on the horse and with your head."

"What?" asked Antonia. "What do you mean?"

"Very simple." Mr. Hegemann stood in front of her again with his friendly smile. "Everything you do with your horse, you have to have thought through and done in your head from beginning to end."

"Ride in your head?" said Antonia.

"You've put it well." Mr. Hegemann smiled. "First, ride in your head; then ride the horse."

Throughout the whole lesson Antonia paused briefly before each jump to "ride in her head." Only then did she feel sure of herself. It really worked!

✳

"Be aware of everything, but don't be bothered by anything." This bit of wisdom Mr. Hegemann passed on to her during their last lesson on Wednesday. Antonia didn't understand it completely, but she noticed that the little bit that she did grasp was important. Her riding teacher was giving her great and wonderful calmness for her first major competition.

The trip to Tostedt was supposed to commence on Thursday right after breakfast. Antonia had gotten some extra days off from school. Mr. Hegemann and Maria had insisted on making the trip two days before the competition because Tostedt was about 130 miles from Rosenburg Farm, and the trip there would be a great strain on everyone, especially on Elfin Dance and Diamond, the substitute horse who would be coming along.

"With Elfin Dance, you never know . . ." her riding teacher had said.

In the two days before the competition, Antonia and Elfin Dance were supposed to have time to get used to the unfamiliar surroundings. Together with Mr. Hegemann, Antonia wanted to take a close look at the grounds and stride them out.

Alexander Rosenburg intended to arrive early Saturday with Caroline, Leona, and Mr. Sonnenfeld, so that they would be there on time for the beginning of the competition. Grandma and Grandpa were staying at home, though.

"We can't all go. Somebody has to take care of the animals," said Grandma. Then she gave Antonia a little package with these words, PLEASE DON'T OPEN UNTIL YOU'RE ON THE ROAD. . . printed on it.

Antonia couldn't be really happy about the day off from school; she was too nervous. Wasn't L Class much too difficult for a ten-year-old? There were only older riders in it, after all. L Class meant "easy," but was far from pony riding. Yes, Mr. Hegemann had said she was a good rider, but what if the commotion of the competition became too much for Elfin Dance?

Immediately Antonia thought of other stories. Once Elfin Dance, or so she had heard, had refused at a trial and just plucked flowers. Leona had died laughing when she heard that. But Antonia was not at all in the mood for giggles. She didn't even want to think about how embarrassing that would be.

No wonder Antonia dreamed the wildest things Wednesday night. In her dream, Elfin Dance refused!

He took the gate and the oxer, stopped suddenly in front of the open ditch, casually stuck his mouth in the water, slurped, turned around, got up, and acted like Antonia wasn't even on his back. When she fell, she woke up, and the dream was finally over. Her heart was racing, and she couldn't calm down. Distraught, she jumped out of bed, ran through the dark house to Caroline, and slipped into bed with her sister. Caroline took Antonia firmly in her arms and rubbed her back soothingly. Finally Antonia fell asleep again.

✳

Early the next morning, Maria drove the silver horse trailer onto the farm and led Diamond by the halter up the ramp inside.

"Go get Elfin Dance," she called to Antonia over her shoulder. "He's really riled up."

Antonia hurried to Elfin Dance's stall, and yup! Running from right to left, neighing loudly, he didn't want any halter put on him.

Antonia broke out in a sweat. But all of a sudden she remembered Mr. Hegemann's words: "Don't be bothered by anything." She took deep breaths as she slowly approached Elfin Dance and began, in her singsong voice, to talk to him. "Come, my dear! Here we go now. The two of us will show everybody what we can do."

But the pounding of her heart inside her became more intense. Were doubts setting in?

Again, Antonia breathed deeply. The pounding of her heart let up.

Finally Elfin Dance let himself be led to the horse trailer.

"Can't I just ride in the stall?" asked Antonia. "Then I can keep an eye this crazy horse better and see that he doesn't pull the blanket off Diamond."

But that wasn't allowed. Escorts in the stalls during the trip were strictly forbidden.

Finally the horses were in the trailer, and everyone hugged Antonia and wished her good luck. Even Leona had come to say good-bye, although she would be there on Saturday.

"For the trip," she said softly to Antonia and pressed a small gift into her hand.

"Thank you," answered Antonia, touched. She

climbed into the back seat and buckled up. Maria pulled the trailer out of the driveway, and Antonia rolled down the side window. She waved until there was nobody left to be seen. At the same time, she briefly took in her hand the little rose quartz elf that she had been wearing on a chain around her neck for some time. Elfin Dance and an elf. Maria had given her the elf during the summer, exactly at the time that Elfin Dance had come to the farm. And it had brought her luck so far.

Behind them drove Mr. Hegemann and Felix, who, as the groom, had to be present throughout the entire competition.

Antonia sighed. *What could be in Grandma's little package?* She opened it carefully. A little silvery horse in jumping position appeared. Antonia hung the little horse on her chain. Hopefully the elf and the little horse would bring her double luck!

Leona had given her a "Competition Journal" she had made herself. On the front, a picture of Antonia and Elfin Dance was glued on; all around the photo Leona had handcrafted hearts, flowers, and stars, and she had attached a horse ball point pen with a red ribbon to the book.

A Failure?

Before they got to Tostedt, they had had to stop several times. But Antonia repeatedly succeeded in calming Elfin Dance. Was he as nervous as she was? After all, it was his first major competition, too.

Once they arrived, they got their hotel rooms first. Felix drove directly to the showground and took care of the horses. In their room, Antonia gaped in amazement: there was a big bathroom with a tub; silk curtains; thick, fleecy towels; and a splendid view of a lake.

She let out a "wow."

"But we won't be getting a lot of use out of it," Maria said and looked at her mischievously. "Horses are the order of the day. Horses—nothing but horses! And now we have to get back to our two darlings."

They drove to the showground, where Felix had put up the horses in their new quarters.

"Wow!" Antonia exclaimed again. She was overwhelmed by the spacious facilities: stadium seating, a big area for the show jumping course, and extensive warm-up areas.

The stalls were roomy and the atmosphere friendly, even though a certain tension lay over everything because of the upcoming competition.

Elfin Dance had been visibly nervous when he came out of the trailer, Felix told them. For that reason Mr. Hegemann suggested that Antonia ride a lap with him.

"He needs to move after the long ride," he said. "Later, we can explore the course. In between, give him a break. He really needs to settle in and get used to the new surroundings. I'm taking care of Diamond."

"I'll take over," said Felix, setting off immediately.

"Good," said Mr. Hegemann. "Then I can stay with Antonia."

Antonia curried Elfin Dance and then put his saddle on. She would have preferred to ride a nice leisurely lap around the showground right away if that throng that resembled a beehive hadn't been there. Here a rider was accompanying her horse; there stood two others checking out the ground. Cars were driving up to the stables;

there were horses that were neighing, being led, held, and others being taken to their stalls. In addition to that, loudspeaker announcements, sound checks, and music rang out. Everything was so loud. And everything was so big and new.

Mr. Hegemann showed her a narrow strip on the edge of the warm-up area. "Get some exercise there. We'll get together again in three hours and take a look at the condition of the area and the ground. Agreed?"

Antonia nodded. She took Elfin Dance's halter and set off on the path.

"You're at a competition," Antonia said to herself and to her horse. "Conditions here are different than at a stable."

It really wasn't the first competition in which she'd ridden, but it was the most challenging and biggest up to now. On top of everything, she was the youngest participant. She and Maria had seen that on the list, and she confirmed it all around her. There were fifteen and sixteen year olds, but none who were just ten years old.

She had discussed it in the car with Maria. "I'm much too young."

"But you're such a good rider," Maria had answered firmly.

"Everyone will laugh at me."

"But not when they see how you handle Elfin Dance." Maria had stayed calm the whole ride. Yet she still couldn't rid Antonia of this insecurity, which made her tremble ever so slightly.

"We'll do it," Antonia said again, stroking Elfin Dance, as she led him for a bit along the fence of the enclosure. She hummed a song and noticed right away that Elfin Dance was slowly becoming more relaxed.

✳

A little earlier than they had agreed on, Antonia entered the showground with Elfin Dance, whom she had already saddled, in order to look over the environs in peace with Mr. Hegemann. They were surrounded by people and horses all bustling around—faces that Antonia knew up to now only from the newspapers and horse magazines, as well as first-class animals. It was really impressive. She, however, seemed so small. Did she really belong here?

But suddenly she noticed that many eyes were directed toward Elfin Dance, as if magic were coming from him—magic that had gripped her, too, from their very first meeting. The sight of this noble horse captivated almost everyone. Elfin Dance, at seven years of age, was probably one of the youngest horses here, but presumably some people had already heard about him or read about him on the Internet or in a newspaper. After all, that's why Mr. Bonhumeur had wanted desperately to own him.

Antonia could positively sense the thoughts of those who wanted to get a look. Each one was wondering, *this extraordinary horse is being ridden by a child? That can't be true!* Now Antonia understood why Mr. Hegemann was so concerned about dealing with fear and nervousness. At the moment, a lot of what they had discussed had completely vanished. She tried to remember and breathed deeply. It didn't help. From moment to moment she felt more out of place and wished she could crawl into a deep hole. She breathed deeply again. Just then, from behind her, Antonia heard a voice she knew well, which threw her for a loop.

"Well, little girl? What are you doing here? Isn't this out of your league?"

It was Alina! Help! Was she also riding in this competition?

Of course, she had been on the list. Antonia had just blocked it out.

Alina laughed maliciously in Antonia's face. "And this fine specimen at your side, who's letting you play the stable boy?" Alina added, topping it all off. She was so nasty!

Maria approached with a young woman who seemed somehow familiar to Antonia.

"Hello, Alina, nice to see you again at a competition. Excuse me, please, if I'm interrupting you two, but I have to steal Antonia and her Elfin Dance. I'm sure you'll see each other later," said Maria.

She didn't give Alina a chance to answer, but instead pulled Antonia along. Antonia saw how Alina remained behind, dumbfounded.

"Thanks, Maria," Antonia whispered softly, but Maria smiled and pointed at the young woman.

"Antonia, I'd like to introduce you to Isabella Ruf. She's a journalist and works for a horse magazine. She'd like to write about Elfin Dance and Rosenburg Farm."

Isabella Ruf! Of course! Antonia knew her from magazines! That's why she had seemed familiar to Antonia. She thought about the little photo that always preceded articles by Mrs. Ruf.

The horse magazine was Leona, Caroline, and Antonia's absolute favorite. They read every issue from cover to cover, and Antonia positively devoured the articles by Isabella Ruf. She always wrote such exciting articles about extraordinarily talented horses and exceptional stables!

And now she wanted to write about Elfin Dance and Rosenburg Farm?

That was great! Sensational!

Rosenburg Farm could really use an article in this famous magazine. In the last few years her family had invested a lot in the farm; ultra-modern stables had been built, as well as a new indoor riding arena. They needed some advertising!

And Antonia knew exactly why she was here. Yes, she was here because of Rosenburg Farm, because of Elfin Dance, and naturally also because she wanted to show that she was a good show jumping rider.

"I've already told Mrs. Ruf a lot about you, Antonia—about how you handle horses, especially Elfin Dance. I've told her about the thunderstorm during summer vacation as a little appetizer, and why Mr. Bonhumeur was so enthusiastic about you . . ." Maria talked and talked, and Antonia was so embarrassed that she hardly knew where to look. Where was Mr. Hegemann anyway?

Isabella Ruf kept taking notes. Then, all of a sudden she shouted, "A wonder child with a wonder horse! Now, you two show me what you can do. Later, I'd like to ask you a few questions, Antonia. Is that all right with you?" And she leafed through her notes and made a few more.

What did Mrs. Ruf mean? Was she simply supposed to ride off with Elfin Dance? She had talked at length with Mr. Hegemann about warming up and that she should never, ever just start riding like that.

Antonia would have preferred to stride out this first lap in the unfamiliar place with Elfin Dance and Mr. Hegemann. Actually, she would rather have had a look at everything first with Elfin Dance in peace and quiet. Searching for help, she looked around for her riding instructor. But he was still nowhere to be found, and Antonia suddenly felt very much alone.

Isabella Ruf was messing up all her plans. And Maria seemed to think it was very important for her to give all her attention to the journalist at the moment. But her aunt was familiar with competitions! And Elfin Dance!

Antonia hesitated. Then she just wouldn't get acquainted with the course until later with Mr. Hegemann.

They couldn't have a look at the show jumping course until the day of the competition anyway.

"Okay," she sighed. In the meantime more eyes turned toward them, drawn not only to Elfin Dance but also the presence of Isabella Ruf.

"Okay, then," Antonia said again, turning to Mrs. Ruf. "It'll just take a moment." Then she strode out at least one part, looked at the first hurdle, and committed it to memory.

Finally she mounted and tried to think about nothing except Elfin Dance and herself, the track ahead of them, and the wide view, just as she had learned. She bent down to Elfin Dance, whispered encouraging words in his ear, and, by putting light pressure on his flanks, let him know it was time to get going.

Antonia felt his nervousness, because she and Mr. Hegemann had indeed gotten him used to the loudness of a competition arena, but not to this swarm of people . . .

Elfin Dance pushed forward and fell into a fast gallop. He was just flying! Clean jumps, no hesitation, no faltering.

Astonished shouts became loud. A hum of approval lay in the air.

But suddenly there was something . . . she noticed it in Elfin Dance's movements. Startled, Antonia wondered what it was.

Then the unbelievable happened. Elfin Dance refused; worse yet, he reared, left Antonia hanging helpless in the saddle, and then . . .

The world stood still. For a moment. Then she crashed hard onto the ground and felt a pain in her left shoulder. But that was nothing in comparison to the rage that overwhelmed her. How could Elfin Dance do that?

Antonia lay in the dirt. Maria rushed up to her. "Have you hurt yourself? Is everything okay?" she shouted anxiously.

Nothing was okay, and Antonia didn't budge; she couldn't move because of fright and shame.

"Everything's all right; just go back to Mrs. Ruf," she whispered softly, accepting Maria's help and standing up carefully.

"Are you absolutely sure?" asked Maria, and when Antonia said yes, she turned back to the journalist.

Antonia could have howled, and Elfin Dance merely turned around and nibbled a bit in a flower pot. It was just like in her nightmare.

He had never done that—thrown her off and made her look ridiculous, like a beginner!

When she finally glanced around, she was looking directly into Alina's evil, laughing face.

"I told you, you're out of your league," she said gloatingly, then turned and left.

Antonia took Elfin Dance by the reins and left the arena, hanging her head.

Now What?

So that was it, then!

Antonia and Elfin Dance reached the stall, under everyone's gaze, or at least it felt like that. She was terribly ashamed.

While she was unsaddling Elfin Dance, she thought of Maria. Maria was probably still standing on the showground with Mrs. Ruf, waiting for Antonia to calm down and come back to finish the interview.

Antonia had to apologize for that bad performance. So she ran back to the warm-up area.

On the way, an older man called to her consolingly, "Don't worry about it. That's happened to all of us."

A lady wanted to take her hand. "Girl, you did well. Don't give up!"

No matter how kind they were, though, Antonia felt ashamed. Before she had wanted the ground to just swallow her up, and now even more so. What was she supposed to do? She had become a laughing stock! Dazed and completely red in the face, she approached Maria and Isabella Ruf. She arrived just in time to hear the journalist explain to Maria that, under these conditions, she couldn't write an article in the horse magazine.

"I'm sorry, Ms. Rosenburg. But I really wouldn't know what to write."

Tears burned on Antonia's cheeks. That was so horrid! Everything was horrid!

"But you've never been to Rosenburg Farm. You're more than welcome to come, and I promise you, you won't be disappointed!"

Antonia heard the desperation in Maria's voice. If Mrs. Ruf didn't want to report on Elfin Dance, then at least she could write about the farm.

Antonia wanted to say something about the warm-up and Elfin Dance's nervousness. But Mrs. Ruf was short

and crisp. "You see, it would have been a well-rounded article: a wonder child with a wonder horse on a wonder farm. But, unfortunately, the wonder child and the wonder horse are missing. The wonder horse is a stubborn bundle of energy. You understand, of course, that I'll be following the competition. Elfin Dance is unquestionably an impressive horse at first glance. But he seems to be jumpy. Of course, he's young. Nevertheless, it remains to be seen if his temperament is suitable for his career. I wish you luck, Antonia."

Bang! That hit home like a punch. Isabella Ruf had spoken! It sounded like scorn. Antonia could have screamed.

"Maria," she said softly, "I'm so sorry."

"Oh, Antonia, *I'm* sorry. I messed everything up. I was so impatient that I just couldn't wait. You should have been able to look over the course quietly with Elfin Dance and warm up. I saw what you planned to do. What a fool!" She slapped her forehead. "Don't worry about it. I shouldn't have expected that of you two. I have to apologize to you! You know, Mrs. Ruf came right up to me when she saw you with Elfin Dance. I just couldn't resist."

"Too eager," Antonia said indignantly. "Besides, I'm not a wonder child and Elfin Dance is no wonder horse. Mrs. Ruf's out of her mind."

"Yes, I'm so proud of Elfin Dance and you." Maria was able to smile again.

Suddenly her face lit up. "How about you ride Diamond in the competition? He's a pro. Of course, not as sensational as Elfin Dance, but it would be worth a try. Maybe Mrs. Ruf would take notice of the wonder child and the wonder farm. You simply ride and jump so well."

Antonia stamped her foot. "Enough with the blasted wonder child. I'm a child. Maybe even too young for this kind of competition. And maybe I can ride well, yes! But I want to ride Elfin Dance."

Antonia swallowed and tried to hold back the tears. She didn't want to disappoint Maria, her papa, and Rosenburg Farm, and she knew how important this competition was for all of them. But to compete on Diamond, she felt, would be a huge betrayal to Elfin Dance! She and Elfin Dance had worked toward this day, and now Elfin Dance was supposed to stand on the sidelines and watch her ride Diamond? Just because they had all made a mistake? No! She just couldn't do that to him!

How much she wished Leona were there! She would definitely have an unexpected solution on hand again— and she wouldn't be so crazy. And she would keep her spirits up!

And where *was* Mr. Hegemann? He had such a sure, level-headed way about him.

But neither one was there.

Sadly Antonia went into the stable to find Elfin Dance. "Hello, my dear. Do you know that I'm really mad at you? To refuse is one thing, but to throw me off just isn't funny at all. Such a noble horse, and then you behave like a stubborn mule!"

Elfin Dance pricked his ears and turned his head toward Antonia. He snorted softly and nudged her gently.

"What's that supposed to be? Do you want to apologize to me? That's the least of it! You know what? We shouldn't have let ourselves get involved in that exhibition. We needed to have checked things out quietly. Just the way we wanted to."

Elfin Dance pawed the ground.

"Yes, you're right. We should have looked over everything by ourselves first. But honestly, you'll have to get used to it—everyone staring at you like a wonder of the world. First of all, you're very beautiful. But you'll just need a long time to get used to it. We'll have to keep that in mind, forever and ever."

And all of a sudden Antonia knew exactly how she had to proceed in the future. She *had* gone through everything before in her head, but she hadn't stuck to it.

Just then the stable door opened, and Mr. Hegemann looked in. "Maria just told me what happened. May I come in?" he asked.

Antonia nodded, and soon she was in tears, even though she hadn't wanted to cry in front of Mr. Hegemann.

Mr. Hegemann took Antonia in his arms and stroked her head. "Shh, shh," he said a little awkwardly. "You don't have to cry. Do you want some advice?" He pushed her an arm's length away and looked her in the eyes.

"Yes," said Antonia, wiping the tears away.

"You know, I've seldom seen such a close friendship between a rider and a horse like the one between you and Elfin Dance. Elfin Dance really likes you, and you really like him."

"But then why throw me in the dirt? That was not exactly very affectionate. And it was embarrassing, too. I'm so ashamed."

Mr. Hegemann had to laugh. "That was really anything but affectionate. I can't read Elfin Dance's mind, but I think he's testing his boundaries and he's testing you. He's still young, and he's doing it because he's sure of your affection for him. You love your father, too; nevertheless, you do things that he doesn't like. But you know that he'll still love you. And that's why I'm advising you, resolve this with your wild child; then he'll handle the competition. I'm sure of it!"

He pulled Antonia close again, stroked Elfin Dance on the head, and left the stall. Mr. Hegemann was a confidence booster. A real confidence booster. Antonia stamped her foot hard as if in confirmation. "Yes!"

At that moment she knew for certain: now it was time for her plan. The plan that she had developed with Mr. Hegemann over the past few days. That way she would be able to go to this first major competition with Elfin Dance calm and composed. And she would compete. Even if everyone didn't think she could.

She would draw up a precise timetable, just like she had practiced with Mr. Hegemann. For Friday and Saturday. If they stuck to it, it would give her and Elfin Dance confidence.

Antonia got out the journal that Leona had given her and wrote:

First Tournament with Elfin Dance
<u>8 o'clock Friday morning.</u> I will stride out the field

quietly. I will check out the state of the ground and the poles and will commit all my impressions to memory.

After that I will do the same thing together with Elfin Dance. He should see the flower baskets and little flags ahead of time so that he doesn't get distracted by such things later. Even if the show jumping course looks different on Saturday. I will try to explain everything to him. Elfin Dance and I will plan out all possible sections. I'll ride in my head.

<u>10 o'clock.</u> I'll record it all exactly in my notebook and go through everything in my head several times,

even my impressions of the whole area—for example, the spectator seats. By doing that, I'll imagine how it will feel when we take off and land. I'll recite to myself, "My thighs are closed. . . I'm holding the reins close. . . I'm jumping exactly in the middle of the hurdle." Just the way Mr. Hegemann taught me.

2 o'clock. Only then will I take Elfin Dance to the warm-up area. I'll jump just a little with him on Friday, the day before the competition. Maybe two little jumps, no more. I know that he can jump, and he doesn't have to prove it until Saturday. I won't let anybody talk me into showing him anymore. Under no circumstances!

And in the evening I can tell Elfin Dance while I curry him, "Elfin Dance, that was wonderful. Now we're ready for tomorrow." Then Felix will take over for the night.

That's exactly how Antonia wrote everything down. Everything that was important to her. And Friday went exactly according to plan for Antonia and Elfin Dance.

The Competitor

They were just sitting down to dinner on Friday when Mr. Hegemann suggested, "Antonia, how about if you and Maria take a walk through Tostedt? The weather's great, and when you're in a town rich in history, you should take advantage of it."

Maria thought that was a good idea. Antonia agreed reluctantly. "But just a little walk," she said.

The walk through town, however, did not take her mind off the upcoming event. Posters referring to the competition were hanging everywhere. The whole town seemed to be feverishly awaiting the competition. Even businesses were open until late in the evening. On every corner you could buy souvenirs: plates and cups with pictures of horses, little horseshoe-shaped charms for bracelets, ribbons and miniature trophies, towels embroidered with horses, or bed linens printed with horse patterns. Usually Antonia would have been thrilled, but today she wasn't in the mood. She may have seemed calm, but deep inside she felt a burning and tingling of nerves.

Antonia did buy a little silver charm for Leona, though. She knew that her friend would love this small present, and she collected charms like this on a silver bracelet. For Grandma and Grandpa she bought a cup, not with horses, however, but with big red roses on it. Roses were in fact—after horses—Grandma and Grandpa's second passion.

After they had been gone two hours, Antonia didn't feel like being in town any more. She was warm and all she wanted was to go back.

"Come," said Maria. "I'll treat you to an ice cream. After that we'll drive back."

"Oh, yes!" Antonia was pleased. She wanted to tell Maria about her plans over ice cream.

But no sooner had they found seats in a little ice cream parlor and each ordered a big sundae than she regretted her decision. Because just as the ice cream arrived, so did Alina with her mother and two friends. On top of that, they sat down at the next table. Alina just smirked triumphantly at Antonia and then talked loudly as if she wanted to talk to the whole ice cream parlor. It was clear that Antonia and Maria were supposed to overhear everything.

"Picture it: Isabella Ruf has just come up to me. Because after the unsuccessful performance of that little rider wannabe . . ."

The three girls giggled and were obviously having a great time remembering the scene Elfin Dance and Antonia had made.

The whole thing seemed embarrassing only to Alina's mother. She looked at Maria and Antonia out of the corner of her eye and reminded the three of them, "Shh, not so loud. They're sitting right over there."

"Oh, well," Alina continued, unconcerned, without lowering her voice, "at any rate, Mrs. Ruf was interested in me and my Majestic. And if I'm good—and I'm sure I will be—there will be an article about me in the next issue. Isn't that awesome?"

The ice cream didn't taste so good to Antonia and Maria any more. They paid and left the ice cream parlor.

"That little witch!" Maria couldn't stop herself from saying it, and, turning to Antonia, asked her, "What do you want to do? Wouldn't you rather try competing with Diamond?"

Antonia shook her head. *Please, not that again. All because that pain in the neck had shown up.*

"You do want to compete, don't you?" There was fear and worry in Maria's voice. "I don't want to push you, but if you don't want to compete . . ."

Why ask such a question? Antonia knew what she wanted. Hadn't Grandpa always said, "Nothing ventured, nothing gained"? And she wanted to venture, and maybe, yes, maybe, win. And her aunt knew that, too.

Antonia seized the opportunity to finally tell Maria about her schedule for the day of the competition.

Maria was impressed. "Where did you get such great ideas?"

"Mr. Hegemann taught me all that," said Antonia. "He plans out his competitions completely from the moment he gets up, through warm-ups, and until dinner. And he's right. It makes you feel more secure."

Maria took Antonia in her arms. "Antonia, you are the spunkiest girl I know. You'll handle this competition with flying colors."

They went back to the hotel.

Before falling asleep, Antonia thought through her whole plan one more time. Yes, everything would be fine!

The Decision

Antonia woke up very early on Saturday. She picked up the journal and read over it one more time. In her mind she went over the show jumping course step by step—riding it in her head.

There was just one problem: she had to have a quiet little place so she could carefully warm Elfin Dance up. She had found such a spot on the edge of the show-ground, but would Mr. Hegemann and Maria let her go there? Right before the start, they definitely would want to have everything completely under control. That would mean she would have to spend time dealing with Elfin Dance in the middle of the bustle of all of those waiting to compete. But her sensitive and temperamental Elfin Dance needed quiet before his performance.

And she wanted to handle it without the help of Mr. Hegemann or anybody else. Just her. So she had to be able to slip away somehow so that nobody noticed her. If Elfin Dance went to the start calmly warmed up—

maybe even having heard his favorite song—everything would go well. That much she knew.

She went into the bathroom and put on the competition outfit, which she had gotten as an extra gift from Grandma and Grandpa. There was a strict dress code. It even included a satin tie with a silver pin! Of course, Antonia also had to wear her safety vest on the show jumping course. The vests were reinforced at the back so that nothing bad would happen in the event of an accident.

She buffed the gleaming black boots again and looked at herself in the mirror. She looked thoroughly elegant and grown up! Her hair was pulled back in a braid. Just her face had little red spots from all the excitement, which certainly only she and Maria saw.

When Maria came in, she shouted, "Wow, you look really great! Come now, you have to have a decent breakfast." She took Antonia in her arms briefly, stuffed a huge napkin into her collar, and murmured, "So that jelly doesn't spill on it . . ."

Antonia couldn't help laughing. "Hey, I don't need a bib!"

But she left the napkin there, because it would be a shame to ruin the beautiful white blouse.

She hadn't finished her breakfast yet when she heard familiar voices in the hotel lobby.

"Can you tell me where I can find Ms. Rosenburg, Mr. Hegemann, and my daughter, Antonia?"

But before the lady at the reception desk could answer, Antonia ran up to them. "Papa, Caroline, Leona! You're here already!"

"Yes!" Mr. Rosenburg exclaimed and laughingly whirled her around once. "We left very early and there was hardly any traffic on the freeway. And how are things going here? You look fantastic, Antonia."

Antonia quickly slipped her arm through Leona's, pulled her aside, and whispered softly, "It's great that you're here. You absolutely have to help me out today . . ."

"Why, what's the matter?"

She told Leona about the last two days, about Elfin Dance's moods, about Alina making fun of her, and about Isabella Ruf. And that everything had almost fallen apart.

"Wow, Mrs. Ruf is here?" Leona was astonished and immediately hooked. "And what do you have planned?"

"Before the start, I have to get away with Elfin Dance, far from all those people and horses and commotion. I want to be alone with him for a while in order to get him really well prepared. Then Elfin Dance will go along with everything for sure," said Antonia. "The showground is in the middle of a wooded area. Elfin Dance has to run, be free! You know him. But Papa, Maria, and Mr. Hegemann will never let me go alone like that right before the competition. I'll stay inside the

warm-up grounds, exactly according to instructions. I don't want any of them around, though; that's the only way I'll get Elfin Dance ready. That's why you have to help me!"

"Okay, and what exactly am I supposed to do?" asked Leona, not yet totally convinced that what Antonia had planned was really the right solution. But she also knew that Antonia knew her Elfin Dance better than anyone else, and she would never do anything she hadn't already thought through.

"I don't exactly know either," moaned Antonia. "I had hoped something would occur to you. Maybe you could faint or drive all the horses out of their stalls, make a little bit of chaos. But watch out. We don't want to get disqualified!" she added.

Leona grinned. "Well, now you're the one with the crazy ideas. It's okay, something will come to me."

"What are you whispering about?" Maria interrupted them. "If you both want to ride along, you'll have to get in now."

During the ride to the showground, there was unusual tension in the car.

Maria was the one who finally broke it. "Antonia, have you decided on Elfin Dance or Diamond?"

But that was already completely clear. Why was Maria asking again? It was annoying. Antonia and Elfin Dance were already registered, and nobody could just change horses like that right before the start.

Mr. Hegemann was expecting her in front of the stables. First Antonia strode out the course with him. They ran their hands over the poles, strode out the distance between hurdles, and planned the number of steps.

Antonia closed her eyes. "Ride in my head," she murmured and went through the first jumps in her imagination. Then came the second part. The show jumping course was difficult.

"But it can be done," she said loudly.

"Curves." Mr. Hegemann pointed them out to her. "Now, it's a matter of shifting your weight."

Antonia nodded. They continued on. She even took note of flower containers and other decorations. Those were the things that could distract Elfin Dance. Afterwards they met Leona in the stable. Antonia saw the sparkle in her friend's eyes. Did she really have an idea?

One more hour until the start. The horses were saddled, and Leona whispered to her, "You've got to move inconspicuously toward the warm-up area now. I'll distract everyone here."

Just then Leona went out and began to laugh as though she were having a hysterical fit. She laughed so loudly that everyone turned around, and several people in charge even came up to her and told her not to frighten the horses. Everyone looked at Leona, and nobody paid any attention to the girl heading for the exit. A few minutes later, Leona stopped and went to Maria and Mr. Hegemann to tell them where Antonia was. That's what they had agreed on.

Antonia found the riding path on the edge of the warm-up area right away and let Elfin Dance just run. The fresh wind blew around their noses, and Antonia breathed deeply. Their tension fell away immediately.

A bird twittered, in the distance a woodpecker pecked on a tree trunk, and a bee flew around their ears. All the commotion was far away!

Antonia hummed Elfin Dance's favorite song. That got them both going and cheered them up. Elfin Dance was all loosened up. It felt really good.

Always staying close to the showground, she heard her start number called after about half an hour.

"Start number seventeen, please. Start number seventeen to the start, please!"

"Are you ready, Elfin Dance?" Antonia sensed that he was.

And as the number was called out a second time, the two of them arrived at the starting line exactly on time.

Antonia saluted in the direction of the judges, as she had been taught. She felt no fear, no nervousness, but rather a joyful feeling of anticipation.

A murmur went through the completely occupied stands. However, Antonia was barely aware of the crowd sitting everywhere. She was concentrating completely on Elfin Dance and the show jumping course.

"Go!"

The approach to the first hurdles. She needed a fast pace, but she rode with control and urged Elfin Dance on in front of the hurdle.

Take off! Then the first landing. And onward! Elfin Dance pressed forward. The water jump. Elfin Dance hesitated briefly. Antonia's stomach knotted for an uneasy moment. Then her horse cleared the hurdle with grace and strength and galloped on. In front of the last and most difficult hurdle Antonia whispered to him, "You can do it; you're the greatest!" She gave a little help, increased the pace; Elfin Dance took off . . . and landed securely.

"Hooray!" Antonia had the feeling she had done the jumping course well.

Yes, they had done it together!

The Party

Applause burst out! Antonia and Elfin Dance had probably gotten over the hurdles without a fault; she had sensed it. Or had there maybe been a fault Antonia hadn't noticed?

She must have been good, because even though the point judge still hadn't announced any results, the well-wishers were already rushing up to her. Leading the way were Leona, Caroline, Maria, her father, and—a short distance behind, but nevertheless beaming from ear to ear—Mr. Hegemann!

"You two were super!" shouted Leona over and over, taking the reins in her hand and leading Elfin Dance past the cheering crowd. Despite the excitement and noise around them, Elfin Dance stayed calm; he just neighed and looked around as if he wanted to ask, "What's the matter with you?" Obviously he was relishing the attention.

Antonia glanced at the scoreboard. They would

probably get one of the top places. Two riders were still due at the starting gate. One, Alina, was jumping at the moment. And she was darn good!

Antonia could hardly believe it. She had actually gotten through the jumping course with Elfin Dance smoothly. Antonia Rosenburg on Elfin Dance! She looked from the scoreboard to the showground, then from the spectators to the judges' stand. And she was ecstatic.

Another girl was competing now. The horse was fast and powerful, and the rider was riding excellently.

Antonia enjoyed the atmosphere all around her. Little by little she was able to notice details as well, even voices from the loudspeaker.

Taking part is what counts! Papa's creed. How true …

Then she heard her name being announced. "In fourth place, Antonia Rosenburg."

The crowd clapped. She couldn't grasp it. Had she really won fourth place at her first competition in L class? That just couldn't be true! But it was. Or was she dreaming? She pinched herself on the arm.

But then she heard another voice next to her. "Are you disappointed, Antonia? Fourth place is always somewhat the unlucky place, the place without a medal, although you're really very good." An older woman was looking at her in a friendly way.

"No, I'm completely happy!" answered Antonia. And that was really the truth. Although at that moment, it dawned on her how close she had come to getting a medal. Regardless, she smiled at the woman. She was really pleased.

Suddenly a disturbance erupted at the judges' stand. There was whispering, talking, and excited gesturing. Something must have happened.

"I'll go ask what's the matter," said Maria finally. She was just about to go when the voice from the

loudspeaker rang out again and began a long, involved explanation: "Ladies and gentlemen, something rather unpleasant has happened; as a result we have to correct the rankings. Surprisingly, for all of us, a participant must be disqualified."

At that moment, Antonia saw Alina back at the stables waving her hands around angrily; then being pushed along, no, pushed away by other people around her. Was Alina the one who had been disqualified? Even though Antonia didn't really like Alina, for a moment she felt sorry for her.

The loudspeaker rang out once more, ". . . has won second place."

Rats! Again, she hadn't listened to the new rankings that were just being announced.

"Third place goes . . ." the loudspeaker continued. And suddenly Antonia almost got dizzy because all at once she had a hunch . . .

". . . to Antonia Rosenburg."

Cheers broke out. It was as if Antonia were momentarily paralyzed. . . . No, that couldn't be true. But then it sank in, and suddenly she was overcome by a feeling of absolute joy. She jumped up and yelled at the top of her voice, "Hooray!"

The applause just wouldn't stop. The crowd clapped thunderously for the top three winners. And she was one of them! She had the bronze medal! It was incredible!

During the awards ceremony, Elfin Dance held his head up proudly as the ribbon was placed on his bridle. He even neighed.

Antonia congratulated the other two winners.

"We were really lucky," one said.

Antonia laughed.

"Luck, and ability, and the right horse," replied the girl with the silver medal.

"Right," said Antonia.

Only when it was time for the winners' victory lap did Elfin Dance not want to participate any longer. After half a lap, with the exit in sight, he started heading toward the stalls. But Antonia held him and directed him onward. "Oh, no, you don't, my friend." And, sure enough, he joined in the entire victory lap.

She had barely left the jumping grounds when autograph hunters rushed up to her. Girls and a few boys, who held out tickets, postcards, or sheets of paper—even postcards with horse heads printed on them. Never before had Antonia written her name so many times in a row. Two girls wanted an autograph on their arms in marker.

"Now I just won't shower for two days," said one of them, laughing.

Mr. Hegemann popped up between the autograph girls. "That was a great accomplishment." He patted Antonia approvingly on the shoulder and praised Elfin Dance, too. "He's really a natural talent."

A photographer charged forward; flashing cameras, microphones, and jostling followed.

But then Maria arrived. "Could you please wait for

the press conference? Of course, we'll be ready for interviews then."

However the reporters continued to hold out their microphones.

One reporter pushed himself toward Antonia and took her photo. Another wanted to know how long she'd been riding.

"I've ridden since I was in diapers." She answered all questions truthfully.

"And how long have you taken riding lessons?"

"My riding teacher put me on horseback when I was just a toddler."

"Has your riding style changed much because of Jochen Hegemann?"

"I think so—self-confidence above all. He conveys that sort of thing . . ."

She didn't get any further; her father took her hand then and pulled her away.

"Your mama would also have been very proud of you now," he said. "You're very similar to her."

She hugged her father. "Do you know what was up with Alina?" she asked.

Mr. Rosenburg shrugged his shoulders.

"At the moment there are just rumors and nothing definite."

At the stall, in a dense crowd, she met Maria, Leona, Caroline—and Isabella Ruf, too.

"My heartiest congratulations, Antonia," said Mrs. Ruf. "I have to say, you surprised and enchanted everybody here. I apologize for my doubting you! Elfin Dance is really an astonishing horse, and you're a great show jumping rider. Riding in a competition like this at ten years of age is a sensation, an absolute exception. Where do you get all your spunk, girl? Would you maybe give me a little interview right now for the horse magazine?"

"Will you write about Rosenburg Farm, too?" Antonia asked.

Mrs. Ruf nodded and smiled. "Yes, if I may still come, I'd like that a lot. A farm that produces such horses and riders—our readers should definitely know about that!"

"Then of course you can come! How would tomorrow afternoon be? There's a party at Rosenburg Farm then. But, shhh, my father can't find out about it, because it's his birthday. It's going to be a surprise for him."

"Yes, I'd like that, if I'm not in the way? And don't worry, I won't give anything away."

✳

The trip back home on Sunday went off—unlike the trip there—without any interruption. No little jealousies between Elfin Dance and Diamond, even; everything stayed quiet in the trailer. Antonia gave Leona the journal to read. "See, I wrote everything in your great notebook."

Leona was amazed at the plans. "Terrific technique," she murmured. "I'll have to remember that for the next swimming championships."

✳

As they drove onto Rosenburg Farm in bright noon sunshine, they could hardly believe their eyes. Grandma and Grandpa, Mr. Sonnenfeld, Karen, and John had performed magic! In the yard, tables stood in a square, covered with a buffet of mouth-watering cakes, coffee pots and tea pots, and pitchers of juice and strawberry punch.

"On Friday before we left, we set up torches, garlands, and Chinese lanterns. Papa wasn't allowed to see any of it. And we made the table decorations by hand," Caroline whispered to Antonia. "Doesn't it look great?"

And it really did! They had folded little horses out of construction paper and spread them all over the tables; glittering horse confetti shimmered between the plates and cake platters. Caroline, Leona, and Grandma had even baked horseshoe cookies!

Antonia's father was thunderstruck. Everyone gathered around him and sang.

"How did you manage all this?" Her father was almost stammering. But then he got hold of himself again and announced, "Now, it's party time, and we have really good reasons to celebrate!"

Guests arrived from the whole neighborhood. Even well-known riders and show jumping riders, who had trained on Rosenburg Farm from time to time,

came to congratulate Mr. Rosenburg. And Antonia as well, because news of her win at the Great Riding and Jumping Tournament had spread like wildfire. Even Mr. Bonhumeur had called to congratulate her warmly.

"This is the nicest birthday of my life," said Alexander Rosenburg, touched, taking his girls in his arms. "First, your success, Antonia, and now such a great surprise party, too! You really pulled it off!"

When it grew dark, the costumed riders appeared. Felix was dressed as a fiery Spanish woman. He carried it off well and made everyone laugh. Mr. Sonnenfeld rode as a majestic French nobleman, and Caroline was dressed as a princess in luxurious brocade. In addition, there were also a mysterious witch and a magician.

Around the edge of the open space there were torches burning, so that Princess Caroline, Knight John, the fiery Spanish woman, and the imposing Frenchman cast wild shadows.

The knight and the French nobleman fought each other, but the princess and the fiery Spanish woman simply walked in between. Magicians and witches did tricks on their horses, sometimes prancing and sometimes galloping in circles.

Mr. Hegemann observed everything carefully and said, "It's strange. When riding in costume, even the tensest riders relax completely. Is that because otherwise they're afraid of being recognized?"

But nobody answered such a serious question. This was a celebration.

Isabella Ruf kept her promise. During the singing and dancing, which lasted into the night, she had Maria take her around the farm to show her around and explain everything about how the farm was run. She took photo after photo and interviewed people enthusiastically, especially Antonia, who was in the magician's costume.

"You really can do magic, girl," she said.

"But please don't talk about the wonder child and the wonder horse again. That's really not true. A good horse is part of it, but also good, hard training." Antonia was glad she had gotten that off her chest.

It was getting close to midnight when Antonia snuck into Elfin Dance and Snow White's stall.

"Hello, my two darlings." She squeezed up against Elfin Dance tightly. "I wanted to thank you again," she whispered in his ear. His answer was a contented snort.

Then Snow White made her presence known quietly, nestling her nostrils in Antonia's hand.

Actually, all she wanted to do was say good night to both of them, but first Antonia had to tell Snow White about the competition. "And I promise you, next time I'm taking you along and not Diamond. After all, you're Elfin Dance's best friend. And I think if you'd been there, Elfin Dance would have been much calmer from the beginning . . . " Then she yawned heartily—and fell asleep happily between her two horses.